Alina in a Pinch

ALINA IN A PINCH

Shenaaz Nanji

Second Story Press

Library and Archives Canada Cataloguing in Publication

Title: Alina in a pinch / Shenaaz Nanji.
Names: Nanji, Shenaaz, author.
Identifiers: Canadiana (print) 20210301929 | Canadiana (ebook)
 2021030197X | ISBN 9781772602456 (softcover) | ISBN 9781772602463
 (EPUB)
Classification: LCC PS8577.A573 A75 2022 | DDC jC813/.54—dc23

Cover and illustrations by Beena Mistry

Printed and bound in Canada

*Second Story Press gratefully acknowledges the support of the
Ontario Arts Council and the Canada Council for the Arts for our
publishing program. We acknowledge the financial support of the
Government of Canada through the Canada Book Fund.*

 **ONTARIO ARTS COUNCIL
CONSEIL DES ARTS DE L'ONTARIO**

 Canada Council   Conseil des Arts
for the Arts   du Canada

Funded by the Government of Canada
Financé par le gouvernement du Canada |

Published by
SECOND STORY PRESS
20 Maud Street, Suite 401
Toronto, ON M5V 2M5
www.secondstorypress.ca

FSC
www.fsc.org
MIX
Paper from
responsible sources
FSC® C016245

With love to Ayaan, Alina, and Liam Jordan
Dare to dream and believe in yourself
as you reach for the stars

Chapter 1

DOOMED

Nobody, nobody in the whole wide world would believe that Alina would rather meet a fire-breathing dragon than go to her new school.

Alina had not missed a single day of school since kindergarten.

But the Snub in the lunchroom last Friday still stung. Stung her like a zillion scorpion stings. The more she tried to forget it, the more it played over and over like a song stuck in her head.

"Lux, I'm doomed," she told her little cockapoo dog.

"Woof, woof." Lux wagged his tail.

Alina had not told anyone about the Snub. Her parents would never get it.

Mom would say, "Don't take it to heart, Alee. Take the high road."

Dad would nod. He always agreed with Mom.

Huh, easier said than done, thought Alina.

For now, Alina gave the Snub a time-out since her grandma was coming today. Nani was flying to Calgary from Edmonton. She would stay with Alina for three weeks while her parents visited her sick aunt in Kenya. It was why she was cleaning her room. She wanted to show off her new room to Nani.

Dad had helped Alina design it to look like she was sleeping on the soccer field. The green rug on the floor looked like grass, and the top part of the walls and the ceiling were painted blue for the sky. She had used a sponge to add fluffy white clouds. The coolest thing about it was that her bed sat right inside the goal-net attached to the wall.

She put on her favorite song, "Shake it Off" by Taylor Swift, and got started.

Bed: Done.

Books: Done.

She shoved a box of her old comic books under her bed and tossed her dirty clothes into the laundry hamper.

"Woof, woof!" Lux looked at her with his big brown puppy eyes.

He wanted to go outside. "Soon, okay?" Alina gave him a few ear-noogies. She checked the time, counting down the hours until Nani landed in Calgary. Six hours, 360 minutes, 21,600 seconds. Hurry *up*, time!

Nani was like a good fairy with a magic spell for happiness. Her visit was sure to rub out the Snub. Also, Nani was an amazing cook. Alina longed for Nani's yummy homemade food. What's more, each of Nani's recipes had a story behind it.

Lux came up to Alina with his leash in his mouth.

"Okay Luxster, let's go." She hooked his leash to his collar, and they dashed downstairs to her parents, who were waiting for her.

They took the trail that looped around the reservoir in Glenmore Park. The fallen, golden leaves danced around their feet in the cool October breeze. Lots of people were out walking dogs, riding bikes, and jogging.

Lux pulled Alina, almost yanking her off her feet. "No!" She gripped his leash and said firmly, "No chasing squirrels." Lux grunted and trotted on.

This summer, Alina and her parents had moved to a big house in Pump Hill, close to the Glenmore Reservoir, a popular water sport and activity park in the southwest community in Calgary. Mom and Dad wanted to be near the water so they could take walks there every day. Now Alina had a bigger bedroom, her very own bathroom, and a big room for her books. But she had bigger problems too.

She felt lonely and lost in her new school. She'd had so many friends in her old school. Most of them were immigrants, but her new school had very few kids of color. It made her look and feel like an alien.

Alina did try her best to fit in. She stopped wearing the traditional East Indian salwar kameez and wore jeans and skirts like the other kids at school. It didn't help. She had seen a few kids turn and glance at her and laugh as she ate her lunch alone.

Her parents stopped by the edge of a bluff overlooking the water to take in the view. "Hold on, Lux," said Alina. "I want to take a few pics."

She took out her cell phone for a bunch of Canada geese. *Click!* The old steam engine chugging along in Heritage Park. *Click!* The snow-capped Rocky Mountains far away. *Click!* The Bow building and Calgary Tower. *Click!* She sent the pictures to Maryam and Ayaan, her friends at her old school.

Her parents sat on the bench to rest while she and Lux continued along the path. The chickadees chirped in the sky above, and the water whooshed below. Alina loved water. Water was the only good thing about moving here. Soon, she'd be old enough to take sailing lessons.

What a **l-o-n-g** September it had been. The worst part was lunchtime. If the weather was warm, the students ate outside, which was okay. But if it was chilly, everyone ate in the lunchroom, which was a Huge Problem.

Every time Alina walked into the lunchroom, her heart thumped like a drum. Where would she sit? Who would she eat with?

Everyone sat in groups. At one table, four girls in her class, wearing matching friendship bracelets, giggled. At another table, the kids argued about the Flames hockey game. At another, there were kids trading Pokémon cards.

Everyone knew each other. Alina was a newbie. She didn't know anybody yet. There was no room for newbies like her.

She didn't really fit in with any group. She was a square peg trying to fit in a round hole. So, she sat like a loser all by herself in a corner.

The volume in her ears went **up, up, UP**, while her mood fell **down, down, down**. Alina felt like she was watching a big party through a window and she was not invited. She wanted to run away. But run where?

Bits of chatter floated around her:

"Ewww, your lunch smells weird."

"Ugh! What's that? Looks yucky."

"Gross! That looks like wriggly worms."

Alina was glad she hadn't brought Indian food for lunch. She just knew the kids would find it strange and tease her. But she wondered, if she sat alone, how would she make friends?

Last Friday, she had tried to be brave.

At lunchtime, she tried to join a few older kids seated at a table. She spotted two empty chairs. Taking a deep breath, she forced herself to walk toward the table. Every step she took, her legs felt weak and wobbly, as if she was about to fall. Every step she took, she fought with her inner voice that said, *Sit down. Don't go. Don't be stupid.*

As she got closer to the table, an older girl with tons of makeup looked at her and put her knapsack on the chair. Alina moved to the second empty chair. A boy with spiky hair quickly put his hand on the empty chair and laughed. The message had been loud and clear: She was not welcome. *They didn't want her.*

Alina flinched. The Snub was back. The time-out had failed. A black cloud swelled inside her. Her life was doomed.

Chapter 2

ALINA'S DREAM

Now that Nani was here, Alina felt calmer. She even smiled when her parents hugged her goodbye for their trip to Kenya on Sunday morning.

"Hey Lux, today is mess-my-kitchen day," she told her dog. Lux rolled over to show his belly and she gave him a good belly rub.

Alina liked cooking. Cooking was like a magic show. The recipes were spells. The chef was a magician, mixing potions and spices, changing raw food into a tasty meal. She'd even started her own food channel called *Yummy Tummy* on

YouTube, taping her friends from her old school as they cooked their favorite meals. Today, her plan was to record Nani as she cooked kheer, rice pudding, her favorite Indian dessert.

After walking Lux and having breakfast, she asked Nani if she could film her while she made the pudding.

Nani frowned. "Just write down the recipe while I cook," she said.

"Nani, old recipe books are over. Gone. Extinct, like the dinosaurs." Alina sat close to Nani on the sofa and showed her *Yummy Tummy* YouTube show on her phone.

Nani looked stunned. Then she said, "Okay dear, let's do it. Get the stuff for the pudding ready. I'll be back in a few minutes."

Nani came back dressed in a navy blue saree. The silver border on her saree matched her earrings. One end of the saree was pinned neatly to her shoulder.

"Nani, you look like a queen," said Alina.

Nani beamed.

"Can you walk a little, please?" said Alina. She adjusted her phone to film Nani. With each step that Nani took, the perfectly folded pleats of her saree fanned out, and the silver bangles on her arm clanged a happy song.

"Beautiful!" cried Alina, looking at her phone screen. "Go on, Nani. Talk about the recipe for the rice pudding."

Nani looked right into the camera and spoke clearly. "Kheer is a popular sweet dish in the Indian cuisine as the basic ingredients are available everywhere. I will cook the basic kheer, but other variations can be made by adding coconut milk or almond milk or rose water." She set the rice and milk in a big pot on the stove top. She turned the burner to medium-high and let the mixture boil, stirring frequently. "It's important to stir it or it could burn."

Alina was impressed. Nani showed no fear of public speaking. "Nani, you're a natural," she said.

Everybody told Alina that she and Nani looked alike: They had similar features, the same sharp nose, the same love for food. Alina wondered, *Do I have any of Nani's public speaking skills and confidence?*

Nani began to sing a Hindi song, shaking her head and tapping her foot. Then suddenly she stopped midway, her mouth wide open. "Oops, I forgot you're filming me," she said.

Sometimes, Nani did not follow the recipe. She did not use any measurements. No spoons, no grams. Just a scoop of this or a bit of that. She winged it.

When Nani put crushed cardamoms into the mixture in the pot, Alina asked, "How much did you put?"

Nani frowned. "Oh, just a pinch," she said.

14

When Nani added a few strands of saffron, Alina asked, "How much?"

"Just a pinch," said Nani.

When Nani added a few more scoops of sugar, Alina asked, "How much?"

"Umm…," said Nani, trying to remember.

"Just a pinch, right?" said Alina.

They looked at each other and burst out laughing.

After supper, Alina and Nani watched the *Junior Chef* show on TV. Lux lay with his head on Alina's lap. Today's episode was on cupcakes. There were five contestants, three boys and two girls. They were told to bake cupcakes and decorate them, all in under an hour.

"So many flavors of cupcakes," said Alina.

"I have tried about ten of them," said Nani.

When the show ended, the Master Chef announced a new contest for children under ten years old. The contestants were invited to make a simple snack and a drink that was healthy, unique, and delicious. Contestants would be shortlisted based on the snack and drink ideas they sent. The prize was $500.

Alina's heart jumped. She had always dreamt of being on a cooking show one day. This was her chance.

"Nani, I want to enter the contest, but I'll need your help."

Nani put her hand on Alina's back. "Any time, my dear," she said.

Alina squeezed Nani's hand. "Do you know why you're a grandma?"

Nani shook her head.

"Because you're grand," said Alina.

Nani blushed. "And do you know why you're my granddaughter?" she said.

"No Nani, you can't use my answer," said Alina.

"Why not?" said Nani, and they both laughed.

Chapter 3

THE NASTY NOTE

It was nearly lunchtime in school and Alina was really, really hungry. *I could eat an ox*, she thought. Today, Nani had made kebabs with tiny packets of tamarind sauce and coconut chutney. *Sweet*.

At last, the bell rang. Alina rushed out of the class into the hallway where everyone's backpacks hung on rows of coat hooks.

What? A lime-green sticky note was stuck on her backpack.

She read it. It said:

Hey, where do buy your food from?

Pet store? Ruff, ruff.

Alina was stunned. Her eyes blurred. She looked around to see if anybody was watching her. Most of her classmates were chatting and laughing, digging out their lunches from their backpacks. Quickly, she slipped the note into her skirt pocket.

She didn't want to go to the lunchroom. She didn't want to see anybody. Where could she go? Her brain was foggy. She could not think clearly. She grabbed her lunch box and dashed off straight to the bathroom.

Locked inside a toilet stall, she wiped her wet face with her hands. *I wish I looked like other kids. I hate being Indian.* She felt ashamed of her Indian food. Ashamed that she was Indian.

She took out her lunch box and snapped open the lid. The scent of spices filled the toilet stall. The perfectly round kebabs made with

Nani's loving hands stared at her. *No, I can't eat them. Not in here.* She had lost her appetite.

What would she do with the kebabs? She could not bring herself to throw them in the garbage. *No way.* But if she took them back home, Nani would ask a thousand questions.

Slowly, she forced herself to eat the kebabs, one bite at a time. They tasted like chalk.

A voice inside her said, *Go to the principal's office. Show him the note.* But another voice said: *Don't be a snitch.* What should she do?

She was scared to face the principal. Everybody called him the Dragon because when he got angry, he breathed fire. At least, that's what the other kids said.

She dug out the nasty note from her pocket and studied the writing.

The bully had used a red pen to write the message. Clearly, they hadn't figured out cursive writing and had trouble joining the Fs in "Ruff." Who could it be? Why had they picked on her?

When the bell rang, Alina made her way back to her classroom. The rest of the afternoon blurred. She could not focus on what her teacher was saying. All she wanted was for this stupid day to end.

Chapter 4

ALINA IN A PINCH

When Alina came through her front door, Lux leapt on her, barking and wagging his tail. She stroked him, and he licked her face with wet, sloppy kisses. Then he ran around in circles, doing his happy dance.

Nani gave Alina a warm hug. "How was your day?" she asked with a big smile.

Horrible. Alina did not want to talk about the nasty note she got in school.

"Normal," she said.

Nani's silver brows rose. "Normal? Good or bad?"

Alina tried to choose her words carefully. "Pretty much the same as yesterday, and the day before," she said.

Nani frowned. "I thought new things happen at a new school," she said.

Alina did not want to talk about her school, so she asked her grandma, "How was your day?"

"I had a lot of fun," said Nani. "I found a new way to cook aloo gobi."

Alina liked aloo gobi. It was a delicious meal made with cauliflower and potatoes. "That would make a good episode for my *Yummy Tummy* show."

"Sit, Alee, sit. Tell me about your new school," said Nani.

"Later. I have to take Lux out for his walk."

***

During supper, Alina helped herself to a big serving of aloo gobi. She took a big bite, but then she remembered the nasty note. Suddenly, she didn't feel like eating. She chewed, but she had trouble swallowing. It was as if she had a rock in her throat.

Alina's grandma looked at her so she quickly mumbled, "Umm, yummy," and took another bite. It tasted like chalk.

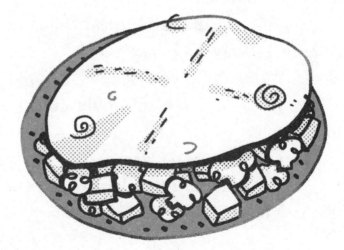

What was happening to her? Whatever she ate, it turned to dust in her mouth. If she didn't eat, Nani would feel bad. Nani would think something was wrong with her cooking.

Alina pushed the food around her plate to make it look like she was eating. She'd make Nani talk to distract her. "Nani, tell me the story behind aloo gobi," she asked.

Nani began. "Aloo gobi brings me fond memories of my mother in Africa. I would go with her on a donkey cart to the local village market to buy fresh cauliflower and potatoes."

"Fun! You should have opened a restaurant," Alina said. "You're an amazing cook."

"In my next life," said Nani.

Alina hoped that Nani would live a long, long life.

"Eat, Alee, eat," said Nani.

"I am," said Alina. But she thought, *I can't*. The rock in her throat got bigger and bigger.

At last, Nani finished her dinner. Quickly, Alina covered the remains of food on her plate with roti and stood up.

Nani frowned. "Alee, you didn't eat. Are you okay?" she asked. Nani never missed a thing.

"I'm…uh…saving it for later." Alina covered her plate with plastic wrap and put it in the fridge.

"Okay, I'll do the dishes. Why don't you rest?" said Nani.

"Thanks," said Alina, relieved to escape but feeling guilty for dumping the work on her grandma.

Back in her room, she struggled to do her homework. She was good at math. But, every time she looked at a problem, her mind re-created the lunch drama at school.

I know, thought Alina. *I will be a spy and find out who sent the note.* She found an empty notebook and wrote the names of her classmates.

The nasty note writer was a mean bully. But who could it be? Alina didn't know her classmates very well, and no one had been very nice to her yet. It could have been any of them. And, if Alina did find the bully, what would she do?

She closed her notebook. She had to focus on making friends. Friends who would make her feel comfortable.

Nani called her. "Alee, TV time!"

They always watched *Junior Chef* together, but today Alina was in no mood for TV. Especially not a food show.

Alina ran downstairs and kissed Nani goodnight. She made a pouty face. "I've got tons of homework," she said.

"How about a head massage?" asked Nani eagerly.

Nani had a cure for every sickness. If Alina was in pain, Nani would massage her head with the stinky yellow Neem oil, and she always felt better. If she had a cold or cough, Nani made hot haldi doodh. Alina called it golden milk because of the color. It was made with milk, turmeric, honey, and cloves. Golden milk was so yummy and it worked like magic. She always felt better after. The drink was even sold as a "golden latte" in some coffee shops.

"Thanks Nani, but not today. I have a big science test," said Alina.

Her excuses stretched out like silly putty, a little further each time. She thought that little lies to keep from hurting someone's feelings were not so bad as long as she told the truth to herself. Well, the truth was that she felt *blah*. All she wanted was to hide under her covers with Lux.

Nani nodded, a pained expression on her face.

Alina felt bad, but she just wanted to be left alone.

Chapter 5

MUDDLED

That night, the Nasty Note played in Alina's mind again and again. She turned and twisted in her bed but she could not sleep. Poor Lux stayed up as well, lying beside her. She cuddled him. "Sorry Lux. I'm all muddled up."

Early the next day, pans clattered in the kitchen downstairs. Was Nani making her lunch? *No, please no.* Alina did not have the heart to tell Nani that she didn't want Indian food for lunch.

The more she thought about eating lunch at school, the more tense she felt. Her stomach was in knots. She did not want to eat her lunch on a toilet seat again. Also, because she'd felt sick last night, she hadn't finished her homework. She could not go to school today. No way. But what would she do?

Lux led the way downstairs.

Nani pecked Alina on the cheek. "Morning, sweetie."

"My stomach hurts," groaned Alina. She doubled over. "I can't go to school."

Nani's eyes narrowed. "Oh dear. Let me check if you have a fever." She placed her palm on Alina's forehead. "Nope. Shall we go to the doctor?"

"No, no, I'll be fine. I just want to rest for a bit, please," said Alina.

"Sure," said Nani. She pursed her lips. "I'll warm up a heat pad. Put it on your stomach. And I'll make some peppermint tea for you."

"Thanks Nani," said Alina, feeling guilty for lying.

Back in bed, she hugged the warm heat pad and sipped the tea. Lux looked pleased that she was home. He bounced around then curled up in a furry ball beside her.

She finished her math homework and fell asleep. When she woke, her stomach growled. She was hungry. "Lunchtime, Lux."

"Nani, Nani, your magic worked," cried Alina, coming downstairs. "I feel better."

"Good, good," said Nani, washing pots in the sink.

Alina hugged her. "Did I ever tell you that you're the best?"

Nani smiled. "And did I ever tell you that you are better than the best?"

"Nani, you can't do any better than your best," said Alina.

Nani laughed. "One hundred percent right," she said. "Actually, it's not about always being the best. It's about being better than you were before."

"I'm starving," said Alina.

"Good," said Nani. "I'll warm up your porridge just right, like Goldilocks."

Nani sat next to Alina at the table. Alina gulped down the porridge until her bowl was clean. "Do you know what I feel like eating for lunch?"

"What?" asked Nani.

"Mogo fries," Alina said.

"Your mom likes those too," said Nani. "Like mother, like daughter."

"Nani, what is mogo?" asked Alina.

"It's a root vegetable like a potato. It grows underground," said Nani. "It's called cassava in Africa and yucca in some Spanish-speaking countries. Do you know it has more protein than potatoes?"

Alina shook her head. "Interesting," she said. "Today, we'll trade roles. I cook, you taste."

"Okay-dokey," said Nani.

"I'm going to cook the mogo fries my way," said Alina. "I won't fry them. I'll boil the mogo, then bake it."

Nani sat down. "I'll watch. The student has become the master."

Alina smiled. She boiled the frozen mogo in a pot with salt, then cut it straight like fries. *Ah!* she thought. Mogo fries would work very well as a snack in the cooking contest. They were yummy, healthy, and unique.

She sprayed olive oil over the mogo pieces on the tray. Next, she sprinkled some salt, chilies, and lemon juice over the pieces. She tossed the tray a few times to make sure all the pieces were coated evenly with spices. Last, she placed the tray in the pre-heated oven for ten minutes.

She looked at her grandma with a twinkle in her eye and said, "Nani, guess how much spice I put?"

"Just a pinch, right?" said Nani, and they both burst out laughing.

Alina made the tamarind sauce and they sat at the table to eat. They dipped the warm mogo pieces in the sweet-sour tamarind sauce and ate to their hearts' content.

"Nice! Crispy and crunchy outside, soft and creamy inside," said Nani.

Alina smiled. "It's nice to eat lunch at home." She wished she could eat lunch here every day, but her parents had a busy work schedule, so she had to eat at school.

Nani rose to her feet. "Now that you're feeling better, how about I drop you off at school?"

Panic swelled up inside Alina. Horror of horrors! Nani was in a salwar kameez, her traditional tunic and pants. What if her classmates saw Nani in those clothes? They'd freak out. Alina would never, ever make friends. *No, no, no.*

"Thanks Nani," she said. "But school's only six blocks away. I can walk."

"Alina, I'll drive you," said Nani firmly. "Any problem with that?"

"Umm, because…because…." Alina could not finish the sentence. She could not think of an excuse. She had run out of lies.

So, off they went to school with Lux and Alina in the back seat. Alina's mouth was dry, her stomach twisting into knots again. As they approached the school gate, she cried, "Stop Nani. Can you drop me off here?"

Nani looked over her, blinking. She seemed confused.

"Please Nani, I'd like to go by myself," said Alina.

Nani nodded, but she looked disappointed.

Alina felt guilty but she was helpless. She gave a quick peck on Nani's cheek, stepped out of the car, and scooted away as fast as she could.

Chapter 6

SUPERHEROES

The next day Nani said, "I made pav bhaji on soft rolls for your lunch."

"Awesome!" said Alina. But her stomach flipped. *The Nasty Note.*

"I changed the recipe," said Nani. "I used beets to add color and vitamins."

"Great!" said Alina. She pretended to check the books in her backpack. As soon as Nani left the room, Alina made a cheese sandwich for lunch. Quickly, she stuffed it in her backpack.

At school, English class was fun. Mrs. Sullivan talked about superheroes and Marvel comics. "Who's your superhero?" she asked the class.

Most of the kids said Spider-Man, Batman, or Wonder Woman.

"Why are they your superheroes?" asked the teacher. "What makes them special?"

A tall boy at the back of the class with a mop of wild curls said, "Because they're super fast, super strong, and they have superpowers." The four fashion girls, who wore matching sparkly headbands today, raised their hands. The one with large blue eyes said, "Because they're super brave."

Another said, "Wonder Woman can pull the sun with her lasso."

A short girl wearing glasses who was sitting next to Alina said, "Wonder Woman can also talk to animals."

Alina thought the most important thing about superheroes was that they protected people, but she was too shy to raise her hand and speak.

The teacher moved on to real-life heroes. She wrote down three questions on the board and asked the class to think about them:

Question 1: Who are your everyday heroes?
Question 2: Why do you admire them?
Question 3: What makes them special?

On Alina's right, a handsome boy with a long ponytail yelled, "This is stupid. Having heroes is stupid. I don't have any!" He flung his exercise book. It hit the blackboard and fell to the floor. The other kids started chattering.

"Lucas, see me outside," said the teacher.

Alina had noticed that Lucas never did his homework and often came to school late.

When the teacher and Lucas returned to the class, he looked a lot calmer.

"Quiet, everybody," said Mrs. Sullivan. She divided the class into partners to talk about their heroes. Lucas's partner was the teacher. Alina was paired with the short girl in glasses, Kim Cheung.

Kim told Alina in an excited voice, "My superhero is my dad. Dad knows wacky stuff. He's a walking, talking Wikipedia. I learn super new facts from him every day. Like did you know it's impossible to lick your own elbow?"

"I bet I can do it," said Alina. "Watch." She tried and tried, stretching her neck and twisting her arm, until they both burst into giggles.

"Okay, fact two," said Kim. "Did you know we're related to bananas?"

"Whhaat?" said Alina.

"It's true! Okay, fact three. Did you know that there are more stars in space than there are grains of sand on a beach?"

"Wow, wow, double, triple wow!" cried Alina. She wanted to know more facts, but it was her turn to talk. She didn't want to talk about her superhero yet, so she said, "My dad's an anesthesiologist."

"Like a doctor?" asked Kim.

Alina nodded. "He puts patients to sleep before surgery."

"Ah yes, Dr. Sleep," said Kim. "Me, I put people to sleep just by singing." They laughed again.

"I don't think I've seen you at lunch," said Alina.

"Mom picks us up, me and Liam Jordan, my neighbor. We've known each other like forever. He's always over at my house or I'm at his. You know him?"

Alina shook her head.

"He's the tall guy who sits right at the back, the smart one who answers all of the teacher's questions. I call him Skyscraper," said Kim. "He's cool. And really funny. He knows a bunch of silly riddles."

Alina nodded. If only Kim and Liam ate in school, she would join them in a heartbeat.

"Okay, class, I would like everyone to write a page on your real-life heroes. The essay is due in two weeks," said Mrs. Sullivan at the end of the class.

***

Back home after supper, the phone rang.

Alina ran to pick it up. It was her dad.

Hearing Dad's faraway voice suddenly made her sad, but she didn't cry. He reminded her to do her homework. He said her sick aunt had gone to the hospital, and Mom was taking care of her young cousins. Alina felt a pain in her heart. She realized she really missed her parents, she wished she could hug them and tell them about the Nasty Note, but she put on a brave face and said, "Dad, everything's tickety-boo." Using one of her Nani and Bapa's favorite expressions was her way of saying everything was fine. *If only it was.*

Chapter 7

THE SOCCER GAME

The next day was warm and sunny, so the lunch-room teacher let them eat outside. First, Alina got rid of her peanut butter and jelly sandwich. She sat on a rock and ate the vegetable pakoras that Nani had made.

Yum! The pakoras were utterly-butterly delicious. Alina licked her fingers. She was glad Nani was here. Mom and Dad had tough jobs and didn't have much time to cook. Her subscribers would love pakoras. She would have to include them in her next *Yummy Tummy* video.

Then she saw the four fashion girls, wearing matching sneakers, staring at her. She was sure they were talking about her.

Are they talking about my lunch?

Some Indian foods had a strong smell. She took out a clove from her pocket and popped it into her mouth. Mom said cloves were like mouth perfume. They kept her breath sweet.

After the lunch break, Mr. Howard, their PE teacher, told them to get ready for soccer.

"Yay!" cried the class.

Alina liked soccer but she was worried. She didn't play as well as her friends in her old school. Nobody could beat Maryam or Ayaan. They were the best soccer players in Calgary, almost as good as Christine Sinclair or Megan Rapinoe!

Alina's class changed into shorts and cleats and ran five times around the field to warm up. Mr. Howard divided them into two groups: Sharks and Whales. Alina was with Kim and the tall Liam Jordan on the Whales team.

"Hey Kim," said Liam. "Who's more powerful, a shark or a whale?"

"Good one," said Kim. "I'll ask Dad."

The game began. At first, Alina was nervous and easily gave up the ball until she heard Maryam and Ayaan in her head. *Stay calm. Keep your eyes on the ball. Go after it. Go, go, go!*

Alina got the ball! She drew her right leg back and slammed her laces into the ball like Maryam and Ayaan did. The ball flew through the air but hit the goalpost and bounced off the side.

After some time, Alina realized that most of the kids she was playing with were average players. She was a good runner and got plenty of chances. Each time she trapped the ball under her foot, Kim and Liam cheered.

Once, Alina dribbled the ball and darted through the players, bringing it close to the Sharks' net. She was about to kick when someone snuck up behind her and tripped her. She fell hard on the field, skinning her knees, and for a moment she felt dazed when she stood up.

The teacher whistled. Foul.

Lucas had tripped her. Alina got a free kick.

But this time she didn't try to score. She kicked the ball forward to Liam. He shot at the net and scored.

"Woo-hoo!" The Whales pumped their fists in the air.

The game ended: three for the Whales, one for the Sharks. It was by far Alina's best day. She felt light and floating as if she was flying.

Kim and Liam walked over to Alina. "Great play!" said Kim, and she fist-bumped Alina.

"Nice pass!" said Liam, and he fist-bumped Alina too. "Hey, take a shot at my riddle."

"I throw the ball as hard as I can," said Liam. "Voila! The ball comes back to me. Even though nothing and nobody touches it. How?"

Both Kim and Alina shook their heads. "How?" asked Kim.

"'Cause, I threw the ball straight up in the air!" said Liam, laughing.

"You're going to die laughing at your own jokes," said Kim.

Chapter 8

SNUBBED AGAIN!

Today at breakfast, Alina made a plan over her porridge. She would turn herself into Alina the Spy at school and find the Nasty Note writer.

Altogether, there were twenty kids in her class. If she ruled out Kim and Liam Jordan and herself, she was left with seventeen suspects. What would a spy do? A spy would observe the details carefully. Write them down in their notebook. And that was exactly what Alina would do.

Why was Nani looking at her? Oh, she was

talking to her. Alina shook her head. "I'm sorry. I didn't hear you."

"I made extra kebabs today," said Nani. "Share them with your friends. The way to friends' hearts is to share your food with them."

Indian food will make me lose friends, Alina thought. But she said, "Thanks Nani. Did I ever tell you that you're the best?"

Nani beamed.

Lux tugged at her backpack. "No Lux. Go eat your own food." Then Alina headed for the door. "Bye! Love you both," she called.

After the morning assembly, much to Alina's surprise, the group of four fashion girls in matching boy-band sweatshirts came up to her.

"Hey. Alina, right? I'm Emily," said one, her pigtails tied in enormous bows. "You're the soccer star."

Alina felt her cheeks warm.

"I'm Ava," said the girl with the large blue eyes.

"Awesome socks, I'm Lily."

"I'm Mia. I like your outfit," said another, her smile a mile wide.

But Alina's outfit was simple. A khaki skirt with multiple pockets (she loved pockets), paired with a white T-shirt under a jean jacket, tall socks (she was always cold), and low boots.

The girls moved on to talk about music. They liked the same Taylor Swift songs as Alina. Alina was surprised at how friendly the girls were. She had been too quick to judge them. Later, she took out her Spy Notebook and crossed off their four names as suspects for the Nasty Note writer.

When the bell rang for lunch, she rushed out of the class. She reached for her backpack before others got out. Just in case....

Oops, her shoulder accidentally bumped into Lucas, the boy who had tripped her when playing soccer.

"I'm so sorry," said Alina, in full apology mode.

Lucas scowled. "Watch where you're going!" He called her a racist name and strode off.

For a few seconds Alina stood rooted to the spot. Her lips trembled. Her chest heaved. Her eyes watered. She felt like she'd been punched in the gut by a hundred-pound gorilla. It really, really hurt. She was, like, drowning in pain.

Yes, she was East Indian. Yes, her parents were immigrants. But there was no reason for the boy to yell a racist slur at her.

Why had she apologized to him? She hadn't even defended herself. She could have said that she was a Canadian just like him.

She took out her lunch box from her backpack and fled to the school field, hoping that nobody would notice she was not in the lunchroom.

It was a little chilly today. The warm spell was over. The magpies cackled loudly. Perhaps they were warning each other that winter was on the way.

Oh no! She had way too many kebabs for lunch. Nani had given her plenty so she could share them with her friends. But she couldn't let anyone see the kebabs. *Especially* after what Lucas had said to her in the hallway. What could she do?

Alina had an idea. She could bury the food! She tried to think of a good hiding place.

Right by the soccer net?

No, that was too easy. Dogs like Lux could easily dig them out.

In the playground?

No, someone would see her.

Then she had it. At the back of the playground was a lone, tall spruce tree that was about a thousand years old. It would keep her secret safe and sound.

She used a sharp rock to dig a hole in the ground under the spruce tree and gave her lunch a fitting burial.

Back in class, she ran into Kim and Liam Jordan.

"Hey, I know you had a good lunch," said Liam. "No need to tell the world."

Alina froze. *What? Did he know her secret? How?*

Kim laughed. "No worries. Liam likes to play detective." She wiped a spot of food from Alina's cheek with a tissue from her pocket.

Alina's secret was safe. She exhaled.

"Liam, tell Alina the riddle of the day," said Kim.

Liam grinned. "So, what did the green grape say to the purple grape?" he asked.

"The green grape said, I wish I was purple like you," said Alina.

Liam shook his head. "The green grape said, breathe, you idiot, breathe."

They all had a good laugh. Alina liked Kim and Liam. They helped her forget her fear.

When Alina walked Lux after school, the insult from Lucas played in her mind. For her, the only way to shake it off was to cook. Cooking always made her feel better.

Back home, she dashed into the kitchen and called for her grandma.

"Nani, I'm going to make a few drinks. I want to choose a unique and healthy drink for the *Junior Chef* contest. Will you be my guinea pig?"

"I'm all yours," said Nani.

Alina scanned the recipes on her phone. "Okay, I'll make rose-sherbet, almond milk with saffron, and mango shake," she said.

What a joy it was to cut and grate and whip and stir, and the best of all, to taste! "Okay Nani, please sit here. Let's do a blind taste test. One, two, three—go."

Nani shut her eyes and sipped all three drinks that Alina gave her.

Nani chose almond milk as her favorite. "The other drinks are way too sweet for me," she said.

Alina liked the mango shake, but Nani was right. It was rich and sugary. *Ah!* she thought. *What if I use yoghurt instead of full milk?*

"I'll make the mango shake lighter," said Alina. She set to work. Presentation was important. So Alina sprinkled a few sliced almonds and pistachios on top of the shake.

She took a few sips. "Yummy." She smacked her lips together. Then she offered a glass to her grandma. "Here, Nani. Try this."

Nani had a little sip. "Hmm, nice. You can call it mango lassi," she said. "Add a scoop of ice-cream to it and it will turn into a frappé."

"Okay, mango lassi it is," said Alina. "It's unique and healthy and yummy enough to be in the contest," she said.

"Now for my *Yummy Tummy* show." She got the camera ready. "Nani, please tell the viewers how mango lassi is made and how it tastes?"

Once again Nani spoke very well. Alina was pleased.

After supper, she got a call from her parents in Kenya. Mom sounded sad. She said Dad's sister, Alina's sick aunt, had passed away. Dad said they were busy with funeral ceremonies and giving support to the family.

Alina didn't know her aunt very well, but having spent last summer with her cousins, she felt very bad that they had lost their mother. Her eyes turned misty, but she tried her best not to cry. She did not want her parents to worry about her. "I'm fine,"she told her dad. "I do my homework every day and am having a lot of fun with Nani."

Chapter 9

NANi'S LOVE STORY

Over the next few days, it snowed and snowed every day, not just cats and dogs, but like snow leopards and huskies. Early in the morning, Alina stared at the white carpet of snow through her frosty bedroom window. The ground was white, the trees were white, the houses and cars were white. A magical wonderland.

Alina rubbed her hands, making shivery sounds. "Lux, do you *really* want to go out?"

Lux wagged his tail. Wrong question. Rain or snow, he was always ready for his walk.

She put a sweater on Lux and ran downstairs to find Nani singing and making French toast for breakfast.

"Alee, don't take too long. It's chilly out there," said Nani.

Alina nodded as Lux tugged her outside.

Back home, out of sight of Nani for a few minutes, Alina stuffed her Indian food lunch into her backpack and hurried to make a peanut butter and jam sandwich.

At lunchtime, armed with her Spy Notebook, Alina snuck to her lone spot in the corner of the lunchroom.

"Hey, cool overalls," said Emily, applying lip gloss. The other fashion girls nodded. They all wore purple-colored clothes today.

Alina thanked them. She didn't have the guts to join them. Once snubbed, twice shy. Besides, if she joined them, she'd have to follow their fashion rules. *Nope. Not going to happen.*

She took out her sandwich. Of course, her Indian lunch lay in her backpack. She'd give it a fitting funeral later on her way home after school.

Taking small bites of the sandwich, she pretended to scribble something important in her Spy Notebook when she was really doodling flower-like patterns while observing her classmates from the corner of her eye.

Opposite her, Angelo from her class eagerly dug his way into a bowl of pasta. But nobody made fun of him or his food. Her gazed shifted to Oliver, the sandwich guy. *OMG!* He had two boiled eggs that he dipped into ketchup and ate. Gross. She'd never, ever do that, not for a million bucks.

She continued doodling. Next to Oliver, Noah worked his way through what looked like potato cakes with basil. Yum, she'd like to try that.

Alina's doodling changed into thick, bold strokes. Other people were eating food from their cultures, Italian, Jewish, whatever. No one called them freaks. Why didn't the Nasty Note writer target them?

People from different parts of the world eat different types of food. Doesn't everyone grow up eating food from their culture? Her roots were Indian, yet she did not have the courage to eat Indian food in front of her classmates.

After school, she buried her Indian lunch under the spruce tree, as she always did. Back home, she walked Lux. The walk stirred up a hunger inside her.

Upon her return, the scent in the kitchen was welcoming and pleasant. What was it? She could not figure out the smell.

"Nani, what's for dinner?"

"Kuku paka," said Nani. "Coconut curry chicken."

Alina took in a long breath. "Smells good," she said.

Nani stirred the pot on the stove. "Back home, we ate kuku paka every Sunday. *Kuku* in Swahili means chicken. The kuku man would come to our house to cut the chicken. It's very popular among Indians in East Africa as the coast has plenty of coconut trees."

Alina recalled Nani and Bapa's photo album. "Didn't you get married there?"

"Yes, in my hometown, in Mombasa," said Nani, tasting the curry.

"How did you meet Bapa?"

Nani smiled a sunshine smile. She kept on stirring the pot. "We went to the same college in Nairobi. Bapa was funny. He'd joke, make everyone laugh. I told myself, this man will make me happy. I hope he likes me. So, one fine day he proposed, and it became a done deal." She cut open the coconut can and poured the coconut milk into the pot.

"Did you have other boyfriends?" said Alina, trying to dig deeper.

"In those days, we didn't date boys for fear of ruining the family name."

"I'm glad you and Bapa fell in love," said Alina.

Nani chuckled like a little girl. "We're close now, but we were very different then. Um...." She paused. "If he was the storm, I was sunshine, and the other way around. Together we saw rain as well as rainbows."

"How romantic!" said Alina.

"Over time, we realized it was important to be yourself and we accepted our differences," said Nani.

Alina nodded, inspired. Being different works. Bapa and Nani had been married for forty-three years. It was okay if Alina was different from other kids and didn't fit in. The only person's acceptance she needed was her own. She had to be brave enough to be herself.

She heard her mom say, "We must celebrate our differences, Alee."

Easy to say, Mom.

Strange, how Alina heard her mom's voice in her mind even though she was zillions of miles away. Her dad's laugh rang in her ears. She missed her parents. She'd have to wait nine more days for them to return. Waiting was hard. *Waiting,*

waiting, waiting. She was waiting for three things to happen:

1. She was waiting to get used to her new school.
2. She was waiting to get on the *Junior Chef* show.
3. She was waiting to find out who the bully in her school was.

Chapter 10

GOOD SPYING AND BAD SPYING

When the school bell rang for lunch, Alina glanced out the window of her classroom. The sun was shining, but it was still snowing outside. The falling snowflakes sparkled like a million stars. Today was her spy mission.

At lunchtime, Alina walked out and strode down the hallway as if she was heading for the bathroom. When she reached the bathroom, she paused, checked to see if anybody was around, then made a U-turn and slipped back into her classroom.

She checked the first row of desks. She opened each student's desk, searched through their books to see their handwriting, and put everything back. Then she moved on to the next desk. Every handwriting was different.

She found a lime-green sticky note inside Kim's desk. *Whaaat?* Just like the Nasty Note stuck to her backpack. It said,

Go back to China!

Well, the bully was an ignorant fool. Kim was Korean, not Chinese.

Now, on to the second row of desks. She opened the first desk when….

"Alina?" Alina almost jumped out of her skin. It was Mrs. Sullivan.

Busted.

Alina's mouth hung open like Lux's after a run. Hot blood gushed to her cheeks, her teacher was staring at her. It was the stare of someone who has caught a thief in action.

But I'm not a thief.

Her teacher stepped closer.

Alina's legs and hands began to shake.

Her English teacher, who usually had a dimpled smile, frowned. "Alina! What in the world are you doing here?"

Shame flooded Alina's entire body. "I…I…." She could not think of anything to say.

The teacher closed the desk. "I expected better of you!" She shook her head. "I'll see you in the principal's office."

No, please, no. Alina was scared of the principal, the Dragon. Her legs felt so heavy she found it hard to walk. She trudged toward the Dragon's den with a horrible, sinking feeling of defeat.

She stood before the Dragon, who sat behind his big desk, his hair spiked up, his fiery eyes staring at her.

Mrs. Sullivan reported to the principal how she had found Alina in the classroom looking into another student's desk.

The Dragon gave Alina a stern look that made her whole body shake. Rivers of sweat ran down the sides of her face.

"This is a serious offense, young lady," he said, about to spray flames from his mouth. "Do you have anything to say?"

"Sir, I'm very sorry," said Alina. She couldn't mention the Nasty Note. Especially not now, it would seem like she was making an excuse. And she didn't want to be a snitch. Then she'd never make new friends. "Um…I had to check on something important."

The Dragon's eyes narrowed. "Someone's property?" he said.

Alina's clammy hands clenched. *Please, I'm not a thief.* But nobody in her new school really knew her. Only her old friends would say that she was honest, always followed rules, always did everything properly.

She was suspended from school for the rest of the day. She had to write a letter of apology, due the next day. But the worse part of all was when the Dragon called home and told Nani what had happened.

When Nani came to school to pick Alina up, she felt so ashamed, so broken, she could not make eye contact with her grandma. Her whole world had cracked apart. She had made the biggest mistake of her life. She had let Nani down. There is nothing quite as painful as disappointing someone you love.

Chapter 11

SHOW OF SUPPORT

Back home, Nani hugged Alina but did not ask any questions. Lux leapt up, greeting her with wet kisses.

"Thanks, Luxster. I missed you too!" Alina said, thinking, *Happiness really is a warm hug from grandma and a furry puppy.*

"How about an Indian head massage?" asked Nani.

Alina nodded. She ran upstairs to her bedroom. She sat on a stool with Lux at her feet. Nani sat on a chair behind her. Alina rested her head on Nani's lap, draped with a towel, and closed her eyes.

"Ayurvedic massage is more than three thousand years old," said Nani. "It's magical. You will see."

Warm oil drops tingled on Alina's head. The oil gave off a garlic-like odor, but she didn't say anything. With smooth strokes, Nani's magical fingertips massaged from the front of Alina's head to the back, tracing slow circular patterns, releasing the tension knots one by one.

"That feels good, Nani," she said.

"Now the temples and neck," said Nani.

The massage over, Nani took Lux and left. Alina stepped into her bathroom and had a warm shower. Feeling better and ready to talk about what happened, she came downstairs.

"I'm making samosas for you," said Nani, spooning vegetables onto the triangles of dough.

"Great! I haven't had samosas since your last visit. Nani, don't fry them. I will bake them like I did with the mogo fries."

"Sure," said Nani.

The baked samosas turned out fine. Alina and Nani had them with chai.

"Alee, I will come with you when you walk Lux," said Nani.

Lux heard the word "walk" and jumped up and down.

They put on their jackets. It was cold outside despite the bright sun. They took the path around the reservoir in Glenmore Park. Usually Alina walked fast, tugging at Lux's leash. But Nani was slower, so Alina matched her grandma's pace. Lux had lots of time, and he sniffed to his heart's content.

"I'm very sorry, Nani. I let you down," said Alina.

"I'm sure you had a good reason to do what you did. Alee, I have great hopes for you," said Nani.

And before Alina knew it, she had spilled out the whole story about her new school, the Nasty Note, and why she had snooped in the classroom.

Nani squeezed Alina's hand, locking her warm chocolate gaze on her. "Thanks for trusting me, Alee," she said. "I'm here for you. Always."

She paused, then continued. "In some ways, I pity this note writer, this bully. They must be hurt. Hurt people sometimes hurt others. Though clearly it doesn't mean we have to accept their bad behavior. Alee, I know you'll find a way to resolve this."

Pity the bully? No way. "Thanks for the vote of confidence," said Alina.

They turned back to go home.

"Nani, if only all of us were the same. Don't you think all the problems would disappear?" said Alina.

"After I married Bapa, I worried how we'd get along because of the ways we were different," said Nani. "Later, I found that I could be who I am, and he still liked me. And he, too, could be who he was, and I still liked him."

"Right," said Alina.

Nani continued. "Along the way, I learned that we may be different, but we're also similar.

Don't we all want to be loved and accepted? Don't we all have dreams and hopes and fears? When we hurt, we suffer the same pain, cry the same tears. We are like balloons flying under one sky."

"Different colored balloons," said Alina.

"'True," said Nani. "But being different from each other makes us special. Being different makes us *us*."

"Nani, I'm finding it hard to feel special right now."

"Hmmm," said Nani, thoughtfully.

Back home after supper, Alina got a call from Kim. Apparently, the news of Alina's suspension from school had gone viral.

"Count on me, my friend. I'm here for you," said Kim.

Alina thanked her.

"Hold on, Alina. Liam's calling me. I'll put him in," said Kim.

"Hey, girls," said Liam. "What's blue but smells like red paint?"

"Don't know," said Kim and Alina at the same time.

"Blue paint!" said Liam, laughing at his own joke.

Alina told them about the Nasty Note she got and how she was trying to check every student's writing in the classroom when she was caught. Kim said that she too got a note stuck to her backpack a few days ago and began to cry.

"No sweat," said Liam. "Detective Liam will nail down the bully. Bet you a million bucks it's one of those blonde girls who wear matching clothes."

"Okay, I win the million bucks. You better find the money," said Alina with a laugh. She told them how she had also misjudged the girls. "They're nice, just fashion-obsessed. Never judge a book by its cover," she said.

"Fine," said Liam. "If not the blondes, or Kim or you or me, we're left with what? Thirteen suspects. I'll nail the bully soon. Easy-peasy."

The support from Alina's new friends lifted a huge weight off her shoulders. She felt good.

Before she went to sleep, she wrote a letter of apology to the principal. She said she was very sorry for going through other students' things. She assured the principal that it would never happen again.

Chapter 12

DIFFERENT AND COOL

Nani read Alina's apology letter in the morning and signed it.

"Today's a new day. Have a wonderful day." Nani hugged her good-bye.

Alina reached school early. She caught a glimpse of Lucas with a hefty man in the parking lot. The man looked angry. Was he Lucas's father?

Suddenly, the angry man twisted Lucas's ear. Lucas howled in pain. The man whacked Lucas on his head, yelling at him. Then he got into his car, slammed the door, and drove away.

Alina was shocked. She felt sorry for poor Lucas. What had he done to deserve being treated that way? She waited in the parking lot for Kim and Liam to arrive and told them what she'd seen.

Later at lunchtime, Alina walked into the lunchroom and right into the middle of a fight between the fashion girls and Lucas. A few chairs had fallen on the floor. Some students cheered for Lucas to win, others cheered for the girls.

Mia was crying loudly. Alina found out that Lucas had elbowed Mia, pushing her to the floor. Nani's words rang inside Alina's mind. *Hurt people sometimes hurt others.*

"Apologize to my friend," cried Emily.

"Never," said Lucas. He sneered.

"Apologize right now!" Emily insisted.

Lucas charged, pulling Emily's enormous pink bows from her pigtails. Ava and Lily ran to Emily's aid. Lucas's lunch tray fell. The food splattered on the floor, and the glass of juice shattered. His backpack flew, and all the contents spilled out: books, hockey cards, football cards, pens, pencils, and…*whhhaaat?* A pad of lime-green sticky notes.

Yes, indeed.

Alina ran to pick up Lucas's notebook. She flipped it open. The writing in the book matched the writing on the Nasty Note she got. Sure enough, the Fs and Gs were uncurled. It looked like Lucas had written those nasty notes to Kim and to her.

By this time, the teacher had intervened and was sorting out the fight.

After school, Alina told Kim and Liam about her discovery. They decided to confront Lucas the next day. Kim and Liam would eat lunch at school.

That night, it was very windy. The wind lashed the tree branches against Alina's window.

Halfway through the night, she had a terrible nightmare. She put her hand in her mouth to find a loose tooth. She wiggled the loose tooth, and it fell out. She tried another tooth. It fell out too. One by one, all of her teeth fell into her palm. She woke up only to realize that it had been a bad dream.

Alina used her phone to find the meaning of her dream on a dream interpretation website. She learned that dreaming of loose teeth falling out one by one meant she had problems in her life, and she would need to talk about them to solve them.

What problems did she face? The Nasty Note. Now that she knew Lucas had written it, she would speak to him politely but firmly and put an end to it.

She also had a problem with bringing Indian food to school for lunch. Every day she buried her Indian lunch under the spruce. Why?

She was ashamed that her lunch was different from other kids'. She feared they would tease her. She was so scared that she was trying to hide from herself. Hmmm…what would Nani say?

Alee, sometimes it's okay to not fit in. Be yourself. Be true to yourself.

Alina had to be brave. She had to have the courage to stand up for herself in front of her classmates. She was a strong, proud, first-generation Canadian with African and Indian roots. Surely, she could be cool even if she was different from her classmates.

Chapter 13

THE CAT'S OUT OF THE BAG

Alina woke up the next morning to hear the weatherman talk about the strong wind last night. Yay, the blessed Chinook was here! This warm wind was named Chinook, or 'snow eater,' by Indigenous peoples long ago. It could melt a foot of snow in a single day. It could even raise the temperature by as much as forty degrees in a few hours.

She looked for her spring jacket and rainboots. The warm wind would soon turn the snow into slush. "No snowboots today, Lux." They ran downstairs.

After walking Lux, she came home and warned her grandma, "Nani, be careful outside. The roads are very slippery."

"Thanks, Mother," Nani joked.

Alina slurped her porridge while Nani packed samosas for Alina's lunch.

"I baked the samosas just the way you wanted," said Nani.

"Thanks, Nani. I'll share them with my friends, Kim and Liam."

Alina made her way to school. The sound of her boots treading on the snow was much softer than yesterday. What a beautiful sunrise! The sky was painted with shades of pink, orange, and red. There was the Chinook arch. It separated the colorful prairie sky from the dark purple clouds.

For the first time, she looked forward to lunchtime. Kim and Liam would be with her in the lunchroom. But during class, the Dragon said through the speaker that they could have lunch outside since it was warm.

When the bell rang, everyone ran outside. Some patches of snow had melted. The school field was a checkerboard of wet grass and slush.

Alina heard cries of, "C'mon, let's have a snowball fight!" The kids began to throw slushy snowballs at each other.

"Over here, guys. There's some snow under the spruce," cried someone.

Alina joined Kim and Liam. Kim explained the science behind the Chinook winds. "Dad said when moist air from the ocean rises over the mountains, it lets go of the moisture, bringing rain or snow. Now the air is dry, right? This dry air sinks and warms as it comes down the other side of the mountains in Calgary."

"How can air warm up so quickly?" asked Liam.

"Dad said the air warms about five degrees for every thousand feet," said Kim.

Suddenly a voice rang out. "Treasure! I found treasure!"

"What?" asked Kim.

"C'mon, girls," said Liam, making his way toward the spruce tree.

Leo held a soggy lunch bag in his hand, dripping with water. Alina's heart caved in. Horror of horrors! It was her lunch. She had buried it last week.

"Yikes, there's more," cried Noah and Oliver, digging through the soft snow with their gloved hands.

Everybody ran to check out the treasure.

Alina froze, but her heart hammered like it was going to leap out of her chest. Her breath burst in and out. Her secret was out. What would she do?

Run, run, run, said a voice inside her.

She couldn't. Her feet seemed glued to the ground.

"Hey, looks like food," said Leo. "Like meatballs."

"I love meatballs!"said Emily.

"Wonder who buried them here?" said Oliver. "And why?"

Both Liam and Kim looked at Alina.

Alina's game was over. She would have to own up. *I must be brave enough to be myself.* She cleared her throat. "Guys, those are my lunch bags," she said breathlessly. "Please leave them there. I'll throw them away later."

Everybody stared at Alina. She felt very uncomfortable. *Run, run, run,* said a voice inside her again. But Alina stood her ground. *No. I must be true to myself.*

Then, a little louder and with confidence, she said, "I buried the lunch bags. I wanted to keep my lunch a secret."

"And, what's your secret lunch today?" asked Liam.

With trembling fingers, Alina pulled out her lunch bag filled with triangular samosas. "Here, try. I have lots." She offered them to Liam and Kim.

Liam took a bite of samosa. "Yum," he said. "There's vegetables inside."

Kim nodded, busy eating. "Delicious," she said.

Everyone ran to Alina. A jungle of palms stretched out toward her, then a rain of voices:

"Trade you my chocolate chip cookies."

"Trade you my chips."

"Me, me, can I try?"

"We didn't get any," said Emily, and the other girls in her group nodded.

"What are they called?" asked Lily.

"Samosas," said Alina.

"Samosas," said everyone.

"I plan to enter them as a snack in the *Junior Chef* contest," said Alina.

"I'm going for that too!" said Angelo. "An Italian snack with a secret sauce."

Now that Alina's secret was out, she felt a lot lighter as if she had unloaded a heavy backpack off her shoulders.

Kim nudged Alina to look at Lucas eating the samosa. He smacked his lips and licked his fingers. Alina fumbled in her pocket for the note. "I believe this is yours?" she said and handed the note to Lucas.

"This too," said Kim, and gave her note to Lucas as well.

Lucas stepped back. "I…I…I…," he said. He turned beet red. "I…I…," he said again. Then he hid his red face in his hands. The neon notes flew in the wind. He turned around and ran away like a scaredy cat.

The day ended with Liam's riddle. "Letting the cat out of the bag is easier than…?"

Kim and Alina shook their heads.

"Letting the cat out of the bag is easier than putting it back in," said Liam.

Chapter 14

INTERNATIONAL FESTIVAL

For once, Alina woke up before Lux did. She danced, singing a happy song.

Lux looked at her with one sleepy eye, like, *What's wrong with you?*

"It's a big day, Lux. I'm celebrating two big events!"

Mom and Dad had at last left Kenya. They would land in Calgary tomorrow.

And, today was the day of the International Festival at school.

Alina wore her lehenga. Her skirt, blue as the prairie sky, had a zardozi stonework border. She put on her blouse, tucked a corner of her silk dupatta scarf on one side of her skirt, and pinned the other half on her shoulder like Nani's saree. Then she put on her long earrings and glass bangles.

"How do I look, Luxster?" She whirled around like a ballerina.

After walking Lux and eating breakfast, she carefully packed the Indian specialities that she and Nani had cooked last night. Of course, she had taped the cooking on her *Yummy Tummy* show. Each item in the tray was neatly labelled with the ingredients, in case anyone had allergies. Lastly, she checked to make sure her essay book was in her backpack. Today, their essays on superheroes were due. She had spent hours and hours writing and re-writing her essay.

At school, Alina's classmates shone like a

poured acrylic painting, each in different colors. Everyone wore their traditional outfits. Excitement bubbled like a shaken soda bottle. Alina's teachers had dressed up, too. Mrs. Sullivan wore a beautiful Cree ribbon skirt and beaded earrings. Mr. Howard had on a tweed jacket and an English flat cap. And Mr. Louis, the Dragon, looked quite elegant and a lot kinder in a French beret.

Kim wore the South Korean hanbok. The two-piece pink outfit had a long, high-waisted skirt and a pink silk blouse with lotus flowers.

"Wow! Stunning," said Alina.

"You look terrific," said Kim.

The fashion girls looked like cute little dolls. Emily and Ava wore skirts and embroidered blouses with red Ukranian boots. Mia wore a tartan dress, and Lily, a Dutch lace cap and wooden clogs on her feet. Poor Lucas, in faded jeans and a T-shirt, stood out like a sore thumb.

Alina knew how it felt to stand out. She nudged Kim and they both walked to Lucas. "Nice cowboy outfit," said Alina.

Lucas shrugged.

"*Come va?*" cried Angelo in Italian. He wore a gray Italian suit with a cute white bow tie.

The biggest surprise of all was when Alina saw Liam. He wore a navy blue sherwani, the long coat buttoned to the neck.

"Aren't you, like, Irish?" said Alina. "Liam's an Irish name, right?"

Liam tapped a finger on his chin. "Hmm, I wonder who taught me that appearances are deceiving?" he said playfully. "I'm a world citizen," he said.

"I have a riddle for you, Liam," said Alina.

I come in many colours.
I can float but I'm not a swimmer.

I have a string tail but I'm not a kite.
I am seen on birthdays, but I'm not a candle.
What am I?

"Balloons!" said Liam and Kim together.

In English class, Mrs. Sullivan chose three students to read aloud their essays on superheroes: Angelo, Kim, and Alina.

Angelo read his essay.

"My superhero is my neighbor, Antonio. I've met many kind people but no one is like Antonio.

"Antonio is a snow angel. During snowstorms, he gives surprise presents to people by cleaning up their driveways.

"Antonio is also kind to animals. He fostered five puppies from the shelter instead of buying from a breeder."

Then it was Kim's turn. "My superhero is my father. He was born in a tiny village in Korea to a poor family of farmers. He loved to learn, but his parents pulled him out of school because they needed his help on the rice farm. My father never forgot that. He sacrificed everything for his family. He moved to Canada because he wanted us to have better lives.

"My dad and I are best friends. I learn from him every day. He's a fact-finder, and he digs up wacky facts like, did you know the color of hippos' milk is pink? Or that caterpillars have twelve eyes? And that dogs can smell a hundred thousand times better than humans?"

Now it was Alina's turn to read. She read her essay in a strong voice like Nani's in the *Yummy Tummy* shows.

"My superhero is my grandma. I call her Nani. I'm very proud of my Nani. She came to Canada as a refugee with just the clothes on her back.

"I learn from my Nani every day. A Big Thing I learned from her is that we are all the same, yet different: 'different colored balloons flying under one sky.' We look different, dress different, speak different languages, eat different foods, but we breathe the same air, feel the same pain, and cry the same tears. Each one of us has hopes, fears, and dreams. We all want love and to be accepted.

"My Nani is not only a terrific cook but she's also bubbly, fun, and good at everything. I mean everything. I hope I grow up to be like her."

"Great job, people!" said Mrs. Sullivan. She smiled her dimpled smile.

Alina knew that she had been forgiven for snooping in the classroom.

And when it was lunchtime, she ran in the hallway to get her Indian specialities to share with everyone. There were samosas, mogo fries, and orange coils of sweet jalebi. After her classmates had eaten, she would ask what snack they had liked better, samosas or mogo fries. She would enter the most popular snack in the contest.

Whaaat? A lime-green sticky note was stuck on her backpack. It said,

I am sorry.

The note was unsigned. Alina turned around and saw that Kim held a similar note in her hand.

The day ended with Alina writing a note to herself.

You were so right, Mom, about taking the high road.

Chapter 15

THE CONTEST

When Alina came home from school, Nani stood at the door, waving an envelope at her.

Alina checked the front of the envelope. It read, The *Junior Chef* Contest.

With trembling hands, she tore open the envelope.

She read the letter.

Yipeee! Alina was one of the five contestants short-listed for the contest. It would be held at the International Hotel in downtown Calgary next week on Saturday. And the contest would be filmed and shown on TV.

She pressed the letter to her chest. Her dream had come true. She could not contain her joy. Tears ran down her cheeks.

She hugged Nani. They broke into a dance with Lux bouncing around them and barking, probably wondering what was going on.

"Alee, did I ever tell you that you're the best?" said Nani.

Alina felt a warm blush rise to her cheeks. She texted the good news to her parents, as well as to her friends in her old school, and to Kim and Liam in her new one. She wondered if Angelo had made it.

★★★

The next day, Alina took her letter to school. She showed it to Kim and Liam, who passed it round. When Angelo walked in to class, he waved his letter like a flag.

"I got in, I got in!" he cried. "Did you?" he asked Alina.

Alina nodded, pleased that Angelo had made it too.

"My snack is arancini, rice balls with a secret sauce," said Angelo. "And my drink is an Italian soda called Creamosa. What's yours?"

"Samosas. And my drink is mango lassi," said Alina. She really didn't care if she won the prize or not. In her mind, she was already a winner in the contest and in her new school.

"Hey, don't forget we're your tasters," said Kim.

"Yes!" said Liam.

"Okay Liam, why don't you try this riddle?" said Alina. She began,

I'm white but I'm not milk.
I'm small but I'm not snow.
I add flavor, but I'm not sweet.
What am I?

"Easy-peasy," cried Liam. "Salt."

"Right!" said Alina.

She smiled. Her lunch dramas at the school had taught her that just as food is easily eaten with a pinch of salt, her new school would be easy-peasy too, if only she took it with a pinch of courage.

THE END

ACKNOWLEDGMENTS

Thank you Astrum, Shaira, and Mahmoud for your support!

Thank you Margie Wolfe and my extra eyes and ears at Second Story—Gillian Rodgerson, Melissa Kaita, and Bronte Germain.

ABOUT THE AUTHOR

Shenaaz Nanji is an internationally published author with twelve award-winning novels, short stories, and picture books. She holds an MFA in Writing from Vermont College. Her novel, *Child of Dandelions*, was a finalist for the Governor General's award in Children's Literature. Born in Kenya, she now lives in Calgary.